THE STORY OF YOU

YOUR LIGHT SHINES BRIGHTLY

BY CAROLYN LEBANOWSKI

ILLUSTRATED BY STACY HELLER BUDNICK

Editing, design, distribution by Bublish
Published by Bold Quill Press

ISBN: 978-1-647048-84-6 (paperback)
ISBN: 978-1-647048-86-0 (hardcover)
ISBN: 978-1-64704-885-3 (eBook)

***Your Light Shines Brightly**: The Story of You* was inspired by Sophia, Ruby, and Penelope, and dedicated to our grandchildren, Rosemary (Rosie) and Thatcher (Hatch). It is written as a reminder to all the children born into this world—YOU can make this world a better place just by being you.

On a magical night, in a tiny town nestled among whispering trees, rolling hills, and the bright blue ocean, a new star sparkled in the sky.

This wasn't just any star. It marks the expected birth of a child whose heart is woven with threads of loving kindness.

A child whose laughter will echo with the melody of generosity.

A child whose every breath will whisper the promise of a better, brighter world.

This brilliant star shot across the dark-blue sky with a beautiful rainbow of colors trailing behind it.

Those who saw the shooting star stopped and looked up in awe at its magnificence. They felt the earth shift under their feet. Something amazing was happening.

In a flash of starlight, a tiny child filled with pure love and goodness was born.

That tiny child is you.

You came into this world on the colors of the rainbow, with a heart pure and kind, and a sweet light of inner goodness shining brightly.

The Guardian of the Stars gave you five gifts, each to make the world a kinder and better place.

As you grow, you will search for these five gifts in gardens, forests, rivers, mountains, and skies.

In the garden of compassion, flowers bloom, just like our hearts bloom with kindness, and teach us to care for others.

Kindness can also be called Compassion. Compassion means caring about how other people feel and wanting to help them when they're sad or in trouble.

One day, you will see a friend get upset when they lose their favorite toy. You will call on your Power of Compassion by going to them, giving them a big hug, and saying, "I'm here for you. We'll find your toy together."

In the forest of forgiveness, trees whisper tales of second chances and teach us to let go of anger.

Forgiveness is giving someone another chance, even when they make a mistake or do something to upset you.

One day, a friend will accidentally break your favorite toy. At first, you will feel sad and angry. But then you will call on your Power of Forgiveness, and it will help you let go of those feelings. You will tell your friend, "I forgive you. You're still my friend."

Forgiveness helps you wipe away hurt feelings or anger instead of holding on to them.

In the river of courage, the rushing water inspires bravery and teaches us to let go of our fears.

Courage is the brave feeling you get when you face something that might be scary or difficult.

One day, you will go to a new school and at first you may feel scared. But then you will call on your Power of Courage by taking a deep breath, walking through those school doors, and saying, "I can do this!"

Courage is not about being fearless. Courage means doing something even when you feel a little bit scared.

WELCOME TO
SKY RIVER ELEMENTARY
COMPOSITION BOOK

In the mountains of generosity, every peak is a gift that teaches us the joy of giving.

Generosity means sharing what you have with others. It could be your toys, your snacks, or even your smile.

One day, you will be excited to open a big box of your favorite cookies when you notice that a friend didn't get any. So you will call on your Power of Generosity by sharing your cookies because you want to make your friend happy too.

Generosity is the feeling you get when you do something kind for someone else without expecting anything in return.

13

In the sky of gratitude, stars twinkle with appreciation and teach us to cherish blessings in every moment.

Gratitude is having a heart full of thank-yous. It's the feeling you get when you appreciate all the good things in your life.

One day, you will have a birthday party, and your friends will bring presents. You will call on your Power of Gratitude by saying "thank you" and letting them know how much you appreciate their gifts.

You can feel Gratitude for big things, like spending time with your friends. Or for small things, like a kind word or a beautiful sunset.

When you look up at the night sky, remember that the Guardian of the Stars gifted you with these five powers, placing each one in your tiny heart at birth.

Remember them and call on them often.

When we offer our gifts to others, our lights shine together and even brighter for the world to see.

As you grow, may you find these five beautiful gifts every day in your words and actions.

Your light shines bright on this day . . . and every day that ends in a Y.

Monday, Tuesday, Wednesday, Thursday, Friday, Saturday, and Sunday!

AUTHOR AND ILLUSTRATOR BIOS

Carolyn Lebanowski is a writer dedicated to sharing from the heart. Her journey began 30 years ago with heartfelt letters to her children, which evolved into unedited and life-affirming journaling. Today, she focuses on capturing raw, authentic experiences, using her writing to explore and express the pain, joy, struggles, and triumphs of life. Carolyn is passionate about fostering connection, integrity, and radical positivity in all her work. Carolyn and her husband Wayne currently reside in Cascais, Portugal.

Stacy Heller Budnick is an illustrator and art teacher based in New York City. She specializes in illustrating for the children's literature market and teaches art at a public high school in Queens. Stacy finds immense joy in both creating and teaching art, often learning as much from her diverse students as they do from her. She is deeply grateful for the opportunity to illustrate books, educate, and give back to her vibrant learning community of teenagers and their families.